by Steve Seskin &
Allen Shamblin

illustrations
by Glin Dibley

afterword by
Peter Yarrow

DON'T LAUGH AT ME

TRICYCLE PRESS
Berkeley

I'm a little boy with glasses,

the one they call a geek.

A little girl who never smiles

'cause I've got braces on my teeth.

And I know how it feels

to cry myself to sleep.

I'm that kid on every playground

who's always chosen

last.

I'm the one who's slower

than the others in my class.

You don't have to be my friend,

but is it too much to ask?

Ha!

Ha!

Don't
laugh
at me.

Ha!

I'm the beggar on the corner.
You've passed me on the street.

I wouldn't be out here beggin'
if I had enough to eat.

Don't think I don't notice
that our eyes never meet.

I was born a little different.

I do my dreaming from this chair.

I pretend it doesn't hurt me

when people point

and stare.

There's a simple way to show me

just how much you care.

Don't laugh at me.

Don't call me names.

Don't get your pleasure from my pain.

In God's eyes we're all the same.

Someday we'll all
have perfect
wings.

Don't laugh at me!

I'm deaf, I'm blind.

Hey, aren't we all?

AFTERWORD BY PETER YARROW

It was a mere four years ago that I first heard "Don't Laugh At Me" at the Kerrville Folk Festival. My daughter, Bethany, who, like my son, Christopher, had virtually grown up with the music of this remarkable festival, walked me over to the Threadgill Theatre for a sunrise performance that would change my life.

Bethany had informed me that the preceding night a remarkable event had taken place at the campfires. Notwithstanding the ironclad convention of having each song followed by the next person in the circle, the near impossible had occurred; unanimously, the circle asked Steve Seskin to sing "Don't Laugh at Me" a second time! History had been made and the word spread rapidly.

There we sat, my beloved daughter, a singer-songwriter in her own right, with her hand in mine, tears running down our cheeks, listening to a song that told our hearts' stories, recalling events that we had personally experienced or witnessed in the lives of others.

Since I have lived a life of social and political advocacy through music, one in which I had seen songs like "Blowin' In the Wind," "If I Had a Hammer," and "We Shall Overcome" become anthems that moved generations and helped solidify their commitment to efforts like the Civil Rights Movement and the Peace Movement, I knew I had just discovered a song that could become an anthem of a movement to help children find their common sensitivity to the painful effects of disrespect, intolerance, ridicule, and bullying; actions and exchanges, which, in the hands of adults, become the basis for active racism, war, and other devastating dysfunctional behaviors.

In the wake of that fateful performance, I have seen audiences at some 150 Operation Respect: "Don't Laugh at Me" presentations to over 200,000 educators and advocates for children, weep, openly or silently, and sing this song as the movement continues to grow and the curricula and video continue to be disseminated for free (thanks to the generosity of the McGraw-Hill Companies and others). In over 10,000 schools and 2,500 American Camping Association summer camps, the seeds have been sown. Over 200 trainings have taken place to make sure those who implement the program have a solid sense of how to approach such work.

Over 50% of the schools in Connecticut have launched the program. Everywhere, the song, the video, and the curricula are enriching similar programs or helping educators introduce such work in classrooms. In all cases, a song stirred them to act on the research-based, but also intuitively obvious premise: When children (and teachers) feel safe, respected, and accepted for who they are—regardless of race, color, religion, the food they eat, the clothes they wear, the country of origin of their parents— they are happier, their academic performance improves, and their teachers report greater job satisfaction and stay in the profession longer.

Beyond that, when our "Don't Laugh at Me" program is introduced and deepens with, or leads to, long-term implementation of allied programs, the culture of the school changes, palpably becomes more caring and respectful, and remains so. Students will, we can firmly recommend, more likely grow up with their respect of self and others intact, be fine participant citizens and, perhaps most importantly, become peacemakers in their hearts.

All this from a little song? Hardly, but the song is doing its part. And without the generosity and gifted talents of Steve Seskin and Allen Shamblin, this extra element, this appeal to our decency and the best that is within our children and ourselves, might never have been made.

This book is part of spreading the message. Read it to each other, marvel at the beauty and sweet humor of the paintings, feel the feelings it evokes in you and your children or your parents, then visit our website for free materials at www.dontlaugh.org, and you'll be ready to sing the song, walk the walk, and join the effort more fully.

I know you join me in grateful thanks to Steve and Allen whose inspiration has provided us with a voice to create a more safe, respectful, and peaceful world for our children and ourselves.

In Peace and Love,

of Peter, Paul & Mary
and Founder of Operation Respect: "Don't Laugh at Me"
Spring 2002

DON'T LAUGH AT ME

McLEAN COUNTY UNIT #5
105-CARLOCK

If you'd like to reach Steve Seskin or hear more of his recordings, go to www.steveseskin.com.
You can correspond with Allen Shamblin at www.allenshamblin.com.

To my wife, Lori,
and our children, Ashli,
Caleb, and Lindsey.
I love you "now
and forever."

—AS

This book is
dedicated to my wife, Ellen,
and our son, David. You fill my
life with love, light, and laughter.

To Peter Yarrow—thank you for
your vision and tireless efforts
on behalf of children
everywhere.

—SS

For Liane,
Kendra, and Sawyer—
my three favorite girls
that love to laugh
at me and I in turn
laugh at myself.

—GD

The authors and publisher would like to thank Searles Elementary School of Union City, California for the quotes on the back of the book.

Text copyright © 2002 by Steve Seskin/SONY ATV Music Publishing/Cross Keys Music/David Aaron Music and Allen Shamblin/Built on Rock Music
Illustrations copyright © 2002 by Glin Dibley

Tricycle Press and the Tricycle Press colophon are registered trademarks of Random House, Inc.

Original version of "Don't Laugh at Me" written by Steve Seskin and Allen Shamblin © 1998 Sony/ATV Tunes/David Aaron Music/Built on Rock Music.

Library of Congress Cataloging-in-Publication Data
Seskin, Steve.
   Don't laugh at me / by Steve Seskin and Allen Shamblin ; illustrations by Glin Dibley.
      p. cm.
Summary: Illustrated version of a song pointing out that in spite of our differences, we are all the same in God's eyes.
 1. Children's songs--United States--Texts. [1. Songs. 2. Toleration--Songs and music.] I. Shamblin, Allen. II. Dibley, Glin, ill. III. Title.
   PZ8.3.S4745 Do 2002
   782.42164'0268--dc21

                                       2002000549

ISBN 978-1-58246-058-1

Printed in China

Design by Betsy Stromberg

Typeset in AdLib, ITC Bailey Quad, Frutiger Condensed, Garamouche, Good Dog Plain, Gothic 821 Condensed, Melior, and Zapf Dingbats
The illustrations in this book were rendered in mixed media using acrylics, pencil, wallpaper, and watercolors.

14 15 16 17 — 14 13 12 11

First Edition